Lindy Blues

The Big Scoop

by *Dorian Cirrone*
illustrated by *Liza Woodruff*

Marshall Cavendish Children

For Blaise
—D.C.

For Nick and Abbey
—L.W.

Text copyright © 2006 by Dorian Cirrone
Illustrations copyright © 2006 by Marshall Cavendish

Marshall Cavendish Corporation
99 White Plains Road, Tarrytown, NY 10591
www.marshallcavendish.us

Library of Congress Cataloging-in-Publication Data
Cirrone, Dorian.
The big scoop / by Dorian Cirrone ; illustrated by Liza Woodruff.— 1st ed.
p. cm. — (Lindy Blues) (A Marshall Cavendish chapter book)
Summary: Fourth-grader Lindy Blues, an investigative reporter, is on the trail of
an ice cream store that disappears and reappears each day.
ISBN-13: 978-0-7614-5323-9
ISBN-10: 0-7614-5323-7
[1. Reporters and reporting—Fiction. 2. Mystery and detective stories.]
I. Woodruff, Liza, ill. II. Title. III. Series. IV. Series.
PZ7.C499Big 2006
[Fic]—dc22
2005037347

The text of this book is set in Souvenir.
The illustrations are rendered in pencil.

A Marshall Cavendish Chapter Book
Book design by Virginia Pope

Printed in China
First edition
2 4 6 5 3 1

 **Marshall Cavendish**
Children

Contents

Reporter Lindy Blues here, Your Nose for News, bringing you the Number One news show in the neighborhood. True, it's the *only* news show in the neighborhood. But who's counting?

Whether it's neighborhood news or a case to crack, Lindy Blues is there — unless, of course, I'm in school.

Let me tell you about my latest scoop.

One

A Message
from the Capital

It's Friday morning and a teacher workday. The offices of the Lindy Blues Network, also known as LBN, are quiet. I take the opportunity to sneak into the research department, which is also my brother Brett's room, to use the computer. Brett does not always understand the importance of the Internet to an investigative reporter. But, fortunately, teenage boys are very sound sleepers.

I start to check my e-mail for news tips. Suddenly, I get an instant message:

Rocketboy [8:45 AM]: come over here quick!!!

The message is from Joshua Becker, a fellow fourth-grader. Even though he is one of my best news sources, I need more information before I call the LBN news team into action.

Reportergirl [8:45 AM]: why?
Rocketboy [8:45 AM]: you won't believe what's missing this time!!!

Joshua's news tips usually involve something missing. I don't know why the Beckers seem to lose so many things. But a good reporter does not ask that kind of question. A good reporter just follows the news.

Reportergirl [8:46 AM]: what's missing?
Rocketboy [8:46 AM]: just come quick if you want the biggest scoop of your life!!!

I notice Joshua uses a lot of exclamation marks in his instant messages. I also notice that he likes his news tips to be very mysterious. But my sources are important to me, so I try to get more information.

Reportergirl [8:47 AM]: where will you be?
Rocketboy [8:47 AM]: meet me at the Capital

That's the Capital H—two trees and a hammock in front of the Becker house.

Reportergirl [8:47 AM]: be right there!

Just as I press Send, I realize I am still in my pajamas. I turn the computer off and dash to my bedroom. I look for my Lindy Blues Fourth Grade Investigative Reporter suit, but it's in the laundry basket. Someone at LBN is not taking her job seriously.

"Mom!" I call several times. I finally find

her in the backyard, kneeling next to some plants. "Why isn't my Lindy Blues Investigative Reporter suit clean?"

Mom lets out a big breath. "I've been busy with these plants all week," she says. "Why can't you just wear shorts like everyone else?"

"Would Katie Couric wear shorts to cover the news?" I ask. Just so you know, Katie Couric, a famous television news person, is Lindy Blues's personal idol. "Would Katie Couric allow her photographer to film her in anything but her best Investigative Reporter outfit?"

Mom doesn't answer. She puts a scoop of dirt in a clay pot and pats it down. She takes off her gardening gloves and gets up from the ground. "Well . . . I have something hidden away in my closet that might work."

I smile. Big time. Hidden surprises are right up there with good news tips. I follow Mom to her closet and watch as she grabs a plastic bag lying in full view next to her shoes. I make a note to myself: "Sometimes things can be hidden right under your nose— or your shoes."

The bag crinkles as Mom pulls out a lavender suit with a mint green top. "How's this?" she asks. "Aunt Caroline gave it to me after your cousin Olivia outgrew it. I was saving it for when you needed an outfit for a special occasion."

"Perfect!" I say. I hug her hard. "Thank you from the entire LBN news team."

Then I remember: My news team! I dash to the bedrooms, which double as the LBN headquarters. Brett, head of my research department, is still snoring. Because he can be very uncooperative when he is awakened, I decide to let him sleep. There is no need for research yet.

But I need my photographer right away. My little brother, Alex, is great with using a camera, but not so great with getting up in the morning. I shake him a couple of times. "We've got a big scoop to cover. Get ready. Quick!"

Alex jumps out of bed and grabs his camera bag. "Let's go!" he shouts.

I've trained him well. Sort of. "Alex," I say. "You're not dressed yet."

He looks down at his pajamas. "Oops."

Because I am a lot faster at getting ready than Alex, I have enough time to pack our breakfast. I grab two boxes of Cheerios and two boxes of apple juice. Then I realize my mistake. I quickly exchange one of the apple juice containers for grape juice. Because Alex eats in alphabetical order, he should have grape juice so he can drink it after he eats his Cheerios. (Photographers can be very eccentric.)

When Alex comes into the kitchen, I hand him his cereal box. Then I tuck the juice box into his camera bag next to Dad's old camcorder and Billy the Beaver. Alex got Billy the Beaver on his first birthday. Billy has been Alex's constant stuffed companion *ever* since.

I make sure I have my microphone and my reporter's notebook. "Mom!" I yell out the kitchen door. "The LBN news team is off to cover a story."

"Okay!" she yells from the backyard. "But remember to be back in time to go with me to your classroom."

I stop short. "My classroom? But it's a teacher workday. Why would I go to my classroom *today*?"

Mom marches into the kitchen with a potted plant in her hand. "Don't you remember? I promised Ms. Blanco that we'd help set up these plants for next week's science experiment."

I cannot *believe* my mom is asking me to go to school on a teacher workday. "But, Mom, where is the news in a science experiment? Where is the excitement? Where is the mystery?"

Mom thrusts her potted plant toward me.

"Look," she says. "How can you get more exciting than this?"

I examine the plant: gray dirt, green leaves, half-opened blue flowers. Exciting is not exactly the word I would use to describe it. I make a note to myself: "Mom needs to get out more."

Mom puts the plant on the kitchen counter. "Just make sure you're back by noon. Ms. Blanco wants you to film the plants for Open House next week. She said something about extra credit."

Extra credit is almost as good as surprises in closets and good news tips. I promise to be back in time. Then Alex and I head to the Capital.

Two

A Missing Ice-Cream Shop

When we get there, Joshua is sitting in the hammock, licking an ice-cream cone. I stand next to him, face the camera, and hold the microphone below my chin. "This is the LBN news team coming to you live from the Capital. Mr. Becker, tell us about this really big scooooo . . . What?!?! Wait a minute! Stop the tape! Alex!?"

Suddenly I've realized something. "Is this the kind of scoop you were talking about? A scoop of Rocky Road? Marshmallows? Nuts? Chocolate chips? You call this news?"

Joshua shakes his head and licks his ice cream at the same time. Some chocolate gets on his nose. He wipes it off and says, "It's not just about a scoop of ice cream—it's a scoop about a scoop!"

"This is getting confusing," I say. "If sentences were ice-cream cones, that one would be a triple dipper. Now, slow down."

A drop of Rocky Road slides down Joshua's knuckles. He licks it off. "Okay," he says, taking a deep breath. "It's the brand-new ice-cream shop, Mr. Hoop's Super Scoop."

"What about this brand-new ice-cream shop?" I ask. "And, more important, why didn't anyone alert the LBN news team about a new store in the neighborhood?"

"I'm telling you now," Joshua says. "It just opened the other day, but it's already missing."

"Missing?" I say in my best suspicious-reporter voice. "Well, then, where did you get this ice cream?"

"From my freezer," Joshua says. "It's left over from yesterday afternoon when I ordered a triple scoop from Mr. Hoop's store. I couldn't eat it all, so I saved some to eat this morning."

Now I am even more confused. But Joshua is a good friend, and I need a top story for tomorrow night when the LBN news show airs in my garage. I turn to Alex. "Okay," I say. "Roll the tape!"

"I am here at the Capital to cover a scoop. A big scoop. A scoop about a missing ice-cream shop."

I motion for Joshua to join me in front of the camera. "Mr. Becker," I say, "how long has this ice-cream shop been missing?"

"About sixteen hours. It was there yesterday afternoon. But this morning, it was gone."

"And has this ice-cream shop ever been missing before?" I ask.

"Not that I know of," Joshua says. "I told you, it's brand-new."

"Have you called the police about this?"

"Yes," Joshua says. "I called this morning. But they told me they wouldn't get involved unless the ice-cream shop was still missing after twenty-four hours."

I see that Lindy Blues will be on her own in this investigation.

"Mr. Becker, tell us when you first noticed this ice-cream shop was missing."

"This morning. I turned on *Lizard Wizards*, my favorite TV show, and one of the lizards was eating an ice-cream cone, and it looked good. So I went to the kitchen and got my leftover waffle cone with Rocky Road. When Amy saw the cone, she said she wanted ice cream too."

So far, this is not hard to believe. Amy happens to be Joshua's little sister and,

14

like Joshua, a big fan of ice cream. Could she be my first suspect?

"Mr. Becker, let's go inside and see what Ms. Becker has to say about this."

Three

The Search for Suspects

Alex follows us inside with his camera. After searching the kitchen and dining room, I move to the living room. I find the suspect in front of the television, eating popcorn. The smell of popcorn so early in the morning makes me a little bit queasy. But I know what I have to do.

I sneak up on the suspect from behind. She doesn't move.

I get closer. She doesn't move.

I get even closer. She screams and throws her popcorn all over the red rug.

I make a note on my reporter's pad: "The suspect seems rather jumpy."

"Lindeeeee!" Amy screams. "You made me spill my popcorn."

"Ms. Becker," I say. "You seem awfully nervous. Could it be that you have something to do with this missing ice-cream shop?"

"First of all, Lindy, the name is Amy, not Ms. Becker. Second, I'm the one who wanted the ice cream and found out Mr. Hoop's Super Scoop was missing. And, third, do you see me eating ice cream? If I had something to do with a missing ice-cream shop, don't you think I would've taken at least one scoop?"

Amy stands and puts her hands on her hips. "And, by the way, you owe me a box of popcorn."

Amy may only be in second grade, but she argues like a pro. I can rule her out as a suspect. But I'm going to need her help, and it might take some convincing. "I'll get you more popcorn later if you help me with the investigation," I say.

"Okay," Amy says. "But I'm hungry now."

A good reporter keeps a stash of snacks just in case an investigation takes a little longer than planned. I grab a granola bar from my pocket and hand it to Amy.

She looks at it for a while and then points to the writing on the package. "What does this say?"

"Gra-no-la," I say slowly. Amy is very smart in some ways, but she has trouble reading big words.

"Gra-no-la," she repeats. Then she tears open the package and chomps. "Not bad," she says.

"So where were we?" I ask.

"In the living room," Amy says. "Same place we are now."

I try not to lose my patience. "I meant, where were we in the story."

"Oh," Amy says. "I was just telling you that I was the one who discovered

Mr. Hoop's Super Scoop was missing."

"And how did you find that out?" I ask.

"It happened this morning. I woke up because I heard the television. Joshua was watching *Lizard Wizards*. I love it when they use their long, slimy tongues to capture the bad guy. And when they . . ."

"Uhm, yes, Ms. Becker, I'm sure you do, but could we stay focused on the missing ice-cream shop?"

"Okay, Lindy, I'm just trying to tell you what happened. As I was saying, I got up to see *Lizard Wizards,* and I saw Joshua with his ice-cream cone from yesterday. It looked good, so I asked him for some. But he said, 'No.'" Amy shoots Joshua a look that would scare a lizard wizard.

"I'm sorry," Joshua says. "But you ate your whole cone yesterday."

"So then what did you do?" I ask Amy.

"I got dressed, put Dakota on her leash, and took her for a walk to Mr. Hoop's Super Scoop."

Just as Amy mentions Dakota's name, the dog bounds into the room, takes her place by Amy's side, and eyes me suspiciously. No one messes with Amy as long as Dakota is around.

"Hmmm," I say. "Could Dakota have something to do with this missing ice-cream shop?"

Dakota growls at me.

Amy scowls. "You know she only eats dog food. Why would she want a whole ice-cream shop?"

Amy has a point. "Well then. Tell me what happened next."

"The ice-cream shop wasn't there."

"It wasn't there?" I say.

"Are you a reporter or a parrot?" Amy asks.

Sometimes a good reporter must take abuse from her sources. It's part of the job. I am about to tell Amy that I am not a parrot when I realize that I have ignored a prime suspect. I turn to Joshua Becker who is sucking the ice cream out of the bottom of what's left of his cone. "Mr. Becker," I say. "Exactly where were you when Ms. Becker was walking Dakota to the ice-cream shop?"

Joshua shoves the last tiny bit of cone into his mouth and crunches. Loudly. I make a note to myself: "Never interview a subject when he is eating."

"I stayed home to watch the end of *Lizard Wizards*," Joshua says. "It was just getting to the part where they catch the bad guy by sliming him with their long lizard tongues."

Enough of lizard tongues. Though I am not interested in lizard body parts, the tongue reminds me of something. "Mr. Becker, was that ice-cream cone you just ate the same ice-cream cone you got out of the freezer this morning?"

"Yes, it was," Joshua says.

Either Joshua is the slowest ice-cream eater on the face of the earth or I am missing a clue. "Mr. Becker, how is it that your ice-cream cone lasted almost two hours?"

"When Amy came back and said Mr. Hoop's Super Scoop was missing, I put what was left in the freezer to save it for evidence," Joshua says.

"Good thinking," I say. "But didn't I just see you eat the evidence?"

Joshua shrugs. "I got hungry."

Although Joshua's hunger would make him a very likely suspect, I rule him out. Anyone who takes two days to eat an ice-cream cone would not have stolen the whole shop.

"Come on," I say. "Let's get this investigation started."

Four

Mr. Hoop's
Super Scoop

Alex walks backward in front of us. He keeps the camera running. "Which way do we go?" I ask.

Amy points down the street. "You go to the end of Flamingo, turn right, walk to the blue flowers like Joshua and I did yesterday, and then turn right again. But I'm telling you, it's not there."

"We'll see about that, Ms. Becker," I say.

Alex is careful not to trip as he walks backward. When we get to the blue flowers, we turn right and . . .

Amy's eyes widen. "Mr. Hoop's Super Scoop!"

"Yes," I say. "There it is. And it seems to be, uhm, not missing at all."

"But it was!" Amy says. "This morning, it wasn't here. There was a post office here instead."

"Are you sure?" I ask.

"Of course I'm sure," Amy says. "Don't you think I know the difference between an ice-cream shop and a post office? I would never eat stamps."

"Well," Joshua says, "there was that one time when you licked the backs of all the stamps in Dad's prize-winning stamp collection."

Amy glares at Joshua. "I was only three years old then. And, besides, the backs of the stamps tasted good."

"Okay, now," I say. "Let's not argue. We have a mystery to solve. Mr. Becker,

26

have you seen the post office Ms. Becker is talking about?"

"No," Joshua says. "I never go to the post office. I use e-mail. Just like you do."

Joshua is right. An investigative reporter cannot wait for regular mail. News travels much too fast.

I look through the big window of the ice-cream shop. "Maybe Mr. Hoop knows something about his ice-cream shop being missing. Let's go inside."

"Mr. Hoop," I say. "Lindy Blues, investigative reporter for the LBN news. Welcome to the neighborhood."

"Thank you," Mr. Hoop says. "What can I do for you?"

Right away I know I can rule out Mr. Hoop as a suspect. First, there is no reason for him to steal his own ice-cream shop. And, second, I have noticed on TV shows that when a suspect is guilty, he covers his face and refuses to speak to reporters. Mr. Hoop seems very happy to be on the Lindy Blues Network. In fact, he is smiling a big smile for Alex's camera.

"I'm wondering, Mr. Hoop, have you noticed anything strange lately?"

"Yes," Mr. Hoop says, still grinning.

"Aha!" I say. I am on the way to solving this mystery.

Mr. Hoop continues, "I've noticed that it has gotten a little cooler in the morning these last few days. Even though the sun is very hot around this time of day."

"That's it?" I ask.

"That's what?" Mr. Hoop asks.

"That's all you've noticed?"

"That's about it," Mr. Hoop says. "Although I have also noticed that it's the second day in a row that this young boy and his sister have come into my shop. They're on their way to being my best customers."

As a good reporter, I could have guessed that myself. "You didn't notice anything else?" I ask. "Like maybe that your ice-cream shop disappeared this morning around eight thirty?"

Mr. Hoop laughs very loud. All the while he is still looking straight at the camera. "The shop's not open at eight thirty," he says. "But when I opened it at nine today, it was certainly here."

Suddenly Lindy Blues is suspicious. "Tell me, Mr. Hoop," I say. "Are there many other people besides the Beckers who eat ice cream at nine o'clock in the morning?"

Mr. Hoop laughs again. "Not many. I open early for the customers who like coffee drinks in the morning." He smiles at the camera. "Have you tried my famous Frozen Coffee Carrumba?" he bellows.

Mr. Hoop's behavior is very odd, but not in a missing-ice-cream-shop-kind-of-way.

I look at Amy. "Maybe you were

confused," I say. "Maybe you just thought the ice-cream shop was missing when it was really only closed."

"I think I know the difference between a closed shop and a shop that isn't there," Amy says. "Besides, I told you, there was a post office here instead."

Lindy Blues doesn't know what to believe.

Mr. Hoop chuckles into the camera. "I'm pretty sure I would have noticed if my ice-cream shop, Mr. Hoop's Super Scoop, was missing."

"Very well then," I say. "I think we'd better move on." I can tell Mr. Hoop will be no more help in getting to the bottom of this scoop.

"Wait a minute," Amy says. "Since we're here, I think I'll try a new flavor." She points to a bucket of very pink ice cream. "What does that say?"

31

"It says Pep-per-mint Bub-ble-gum," I answer. My teeth hurt just saying something that sweet.

"I'll have a sugar cone with a scoop of that," Amy tells Mr. Hoop. "And put some rainbow sprinkles on top."

Mr. Hoop smiles at the camera as he hands Amy her cone. "Here's your delicious ice cream," he says loudly.

Mr. Hoop's odd behavior is clear to me now. He is trying to get free advertising on the Lindy Blues Network.

Amy gets her cone, and we walk back to the Capital. "It looks like our big scoop has turned out to be a big meltdown," I say. "There is no missing ice-cream shop."

"Lindy," Amy says between licks. "I know what I saw this morning, and it wasn't Mr. Hoop's Super Scoop."

"I think she's telling the truth," Joshua says. "When it comes to ice cream, Amy would never lie."

That is something I can believe. But so far this scoop is going nowhere, and I need a story for tomorrow night's news show.

Ms. Blanco's plant project is looking better and better. I glance at my watch. "Time for me to cover my next story," I say. "Call me if you lose anything else."

Five

Ms. Blanco's Garden Clock

Alex and I grab some mac and cheese, or cheese and mac as Alex calls it, before helping Mom put all her plants into the back of the van. When we get to school, Ms. Blanco leads us to the garden behind the science room. I notice she is dressed very nicely for a teacher workday and for planting flowers.

"So nice of you to help me with this project," she says to Mom. "And for you two to film it for me," she adds, smiling at Alex's camera.

"Thank you," I say. "But the camera isn't on yet."

"Oh, okay," she says. Then she picks up a small clay pot and places it on the ground. "We'll put the four o'clock here."

Alex looks at his watch. "Four o'clock?" he says. "My watch says one thirty."

Ms. Blanco points to the small pot. "That's the name of the plant. It's called that because its flowers don't open until four o'clock in the afternoon."

She takes another pot and places it near the four o'clock plant. "This one is a morning glory. Its flowers don't open until ten o'clock in the morning."

After a few minutes, she has made a circle with the six plants that my mother brought to school. I examine the plants. So far, they are not exciting or mysterious. In fact, I am not sure why the Lindy Blues Network should be interested in filming this. But my scoop about the missing ice-cream shop has frozen over. There is nothing left to do. "Alex," I say. "Roll the tape."

"Ms. Blanco, exactly what kind of science project do we have here?"

Ms. Blanco fixes her hair. "Well, Lindy, this is a very exciting project called a Garden Clock."

I look around. Plants are all I see. No clock anywhere. But Ms. Blanco is usually a very good teacher so I let her continue.

"You know how we all have biological clocks?" Ms. Blanco asks.

"No, I did not know that," I say. "Could you explain it to our viewers?"

"A biological clock is like a clock inside your body that tells you when to sleep, when to eat, and when to wake up. Humans, plants, animals—all have biological clocks."

Right now my biological clock is asking me why I woke up early on a teacher workday. So far I have covered a non-missing ice-cream shop. And, now, an overly excited teacher who is trying to make a clock out of plants. But extra credit is extra credit. "Tell me more," I say.

"Each of the flowers we've placed in this circle opens at a different time of 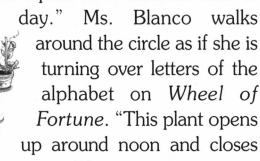 day." Ms. Blanco walks around the circle as if she is turning over letters of the alphabet on *Wheel of Fortune*. "This plant opens up around noon and closes by six PM. This one opens at six AM and closes by noon."

"Please continue," I say.

"Once all the plants are in bloom, we will be able to tell the time of day just by looking at which plants have opened their flowers."

"Very interesting," I say. "But tell me, Ms. Blanco. Wouldn't it be easier to just buy a watch?"

Ms. Blanco frowns. But then she remembers she is on camera and gives me a big smile and laughs nervously. "Well, yes it would. But then you wouldn't be learning about flowers and their biological clocks."

"Very true, Ms. Blanco," I say. "Thank you very much for this lesson in plant behavior." I smile at the camera. "Okay, Alex, that's a wrap."

Ms. Blanco looks disappointed that the filming is over. But when I tell her that I might use her Garden Clock as my top story on the LBN news show tomorrow night, she perks up. "Oh," she says. "How lovely. What time is the show?"

I am surprised that Ms. Blanco does not know the details of the Lindy Blues news show. "Six o'clock," I say. "Every Saturday night in my garage."

Ms. Blanco promises to be there.

Finally, our work is done and we head home. It is time for Lindy Blues to enjoy this teacher workday.

Unfortunately, my biological clock has something else in mind. I fall asleep on the couch.

Six

Missing Again

Saturday morning and the phone rings. No surprise: It is Joshua Becker.

"Lindy, come quick," he says. "Mr. Hoop's Super Scoop has disappeared *again*."

This time I do not rush to get dressed and wake my photographer. After yesterday's false alarm, I am not that anxious to head to the Becker house. I take my time getting ready. Fortunately, my suit is still clean.

I let Alex sleep a little while before disturbing his biological clock.

When we finally get to the Capital, Joshua and Amy are pacing in front of the hammock. "What took you so long?" Joshua says. "This is an important case."

"I am not so sure that it is," I say. "Remember yesterday? We thought Mr. Hoop's Super Scoop was missing, but there it was."

Amy frowns. "I tried to go there again this morning with Dakota. If you don't believe me, maybe we could get another TV reporter to help us."

"That won't be necessary," I say. A good reporter must give in to her sources sometimes.

Joshua, Amy, and I head toward the ice-cream shop. This time Alex walks behind us. He has gotten film of this before. We walk down Flamingo. Turn right. Turn right again at the blue flowers. And . . .

There it is. Mr. Hoop's Super Scoop.

Now I am upset. Could the Becker family be putting me on the trail of a false story?

Could there be another real scoop that they don't want Lindy Blues to know about? "Amy," I say, "are you sure it wasn't here this morning?"

Amy looks very confused. She is ready to cry. But then she remembers the ice cream from yesterday. We go inside.

Amy points and reads: "Pep-per-mint Bub-ble-gum." Then she adds, "I'll have a double scoop on a sugar cone, please."

"I'll have Rocky Road," Joshua says.

I look at my watch. At least it's past ten o'clock.

"No filming today?" Mr. Hoop asks, eyeing Alex's camera.

"Not today," I say. "There is no missing ice-cream shop. So there is no story."

Mr. Hoop knits his brow. I can tell he is trying to think of a way to get more free advertising.

As we are leaving Mr. Hoop's, Joshua gets an idea. "What if Mr. Hoop is making his ice-cream shop disappear on purpose—

to get free publicity?"

"That is a possibility," I say. "Alex, turn on the camera. We might have a story after all."

We stop in front of the blue flowers. "Mr. Becker, please tell me about your theory of the disappearing ice-cream shop."

"Well," Joshua says, "I know Amy isn't lying because I can tell when she lies. Her eyes get squinty."

I look at Amy's eyes. They are not squinty at all. They are big and wide and they are looking at her ice-cream cone.

"There is no other explanation," Joshua says. "It has to be a

44

publicity stunt to get more people to know about Mr. Hoop's Super Scoop."

When Joshua finishes his speech, he realizes that his ice cream has dripped down his arm, past his elbow, and onto the pavement. Alex begins filming the trail of Rocky Road, right down to the sidewalk. Then he zooms in on my shoes.

"What are you doing?" I ask. "My shoes have nothing to do with this story."

"Look," Alex says. "There's Rocky Road all over them."

"What a mess," I say. And I am not just talking about my shoes. This whole story has been one sticky case from the beginning. I lick my finger and bend over and try to clean the ice cream off my shoes. "Stop the tape, Alex. Let's go back to the LBN offices and brainstorm."

Seven

Could It Be Magic?

It is time to consult my computer-whiz brother, whom I sometimes call Brett Dot Com. This is always the most difficult part of a case. I tiptoe into the research department. Brett's biological clock has apparently not realized that it is almost noon. I shuffle some papers and move the mouse around, hoping to make just enough noise that he'll think he woke up on his own.

He rolls over and opens his eyes. "What are you doing, Shorty?" he asks.

"I need some research done on how to make things disappear."

Brett laughs. "If I knew that, do you think you'd be here?"

"Very funny," I say. "But this is serious business. We think Mr. Hoop is making his ice-cream shop disappear in order to get free publicity."

"It's a clever idea," Brett says. "But I don't think it's possible. Unless . . ."

"Unless what?" I ask.

Brett goes to the computer, types in "how to make things disappear," and then clicks the mouse. "Look," he says. "One way to make things disappear is called sleight-of-hand. You slip the object into your other hand when no one is looking."

I stare at the computer screen. A magician is holding a coin behind someone's ear. "This might work for coins and ears," I say, "but I'm talking about an ice-cream shop. I don't think Mr. Hoop's hand is big enough to hide that."

Brett types and clicks the mouse some more. Suddenly I realize there is something

even more mysterious than a disappearing ice-cream shop: My research department is being very cooperative. "So why are you so interested in helping me this time?" I ask.

Brett smiles. "Let's just say I've grown to appreciate the Lindy Blues Network and its Saturday night news show in the garage."

"That wouldn't have anything to do with Kristin Carlucci being a regular member of the LBN live audience, would it?" I ask.

Kristin Carlucci happens to be a cheerleader at the high school as well as a fan of the Lindy Blues Network.

"Maybe," Brett says as he clicks the mouse again.

The words *Disappearing Sibling* and *Magic Chamber* appear on the screen.

"Are you sure you're not being nice to me just so you can make me disappear?" I ask.

Brett laughs. "No, Shorty. Really. I just found this. It's a box you can construct to make it look like someone's disappeared, but they really haven't."

I look at the screen along with Brett. "Aha!" I say. "The box has a false bottom."

"That's right," Brett says. "It's all a trick. Magicians don't really make things disappear."

I think about that for a second. Mr. Hoop would need an awfully big Magic Chamber to make the ice-cream shop disappear. "Do you think there's a box big enough to hold Mr. Hoop's store?"

"Maybe," Brett says. He presses a few more keys, and a very mysterious-looking man appears on the screen. "See this guy? He can make whole buildings disappear. I've seen him on television. Maybe Mr. Hoop is a professional magician too."

"I don't think so," I say. "If he was that good of a magician, he wouldn't need the publicity for his ice-cream shop."

"Sorry we didn't find anything," Brett says. "But you'll still do your news show, won't you?"

I suspect Brett is more interested in seeing Kristin Carlucci than he is in cracking my case. "The news must go on," I say. "See you at six."

Eight

More Suspects

Brett may not have helped me with the case, but he has given me an idea. I realize I have overlooked several suspects. I know what I must do now: Search the neighborhood for more clues. "Alex," I say, "grab your camera."

My first stop is the home of Will and Miranda Malone. As Alex and I approach the house, I notice that all the blinds are shut and the house is very quiet. I knock on the door.

Will Malone opens it slowly and whispers, "Hi, Lindy."

This is odd behavior. Will's voice is usually very loud. I peek through the door. His sister, Miranda, is sitting on the couch with a book. Also strange behavior. She is usually practicing her flips in the backyard or walking on her hands.

"Alex," I whisper, "try to get some film of Miranda sitting still. That is something our viewers have never seen before." Alex moves closer and sticks the lens through the door.

While Alex films a non-moving Miranda, I whisper to Will, "Do you know anything about Mr. Hoop's Super Scoop?"

"Yes," he whispers. "They have very good Mint Chocolate Chip ice cream."

"Good to know," I say. "But have you noticed that the shop has been missing?"

Will looks at me as if I'm crazy. "If it was missing, how would I know it had good Mint Chocolate Chip ice cream?"

He has a point. "One more thing," I say. "Why are we whispering?"

"My mom is taking a nap."

I look at my watch. It is three thirty. I think Mrs. Malone might need new batteries in her biological clock.

I notice Alex is still filming Miranda. "Okay," I say, "I think we have enough film of Miranda now."

Alex blushes.

"See you in the garage at six?" I ask Will.

He gives me a quiet thumbs up.

My next stop is the Carlucci house. Kristin Carlucci answers the door. She smiles at me and says cheerfully, "What can I do for you, Ms. Blues?"

I can see why Brett likes her.

"I am searching for clues to a disappearing ice-cream shop. Do you know anything about the new ice-cream shop in the neighborhood, Mr. Hoop's Super Scoop?"

Kristin steps outside and closes the door behind her. "I wish I could help you," she whispers. "But my mom is on another one of her diets, and ice cream is a dirty word in this house."

Ice cream would actually be two dirty words, but that is not important. What is important is that my news show will be on in just a couple of hours, and I still do not know the answer to this mystery.

Kristin smiles at me again. "Will your brother be at your news show tonight?" she asks.

I assure her that Brett will be there.

Alex and I check a few more houses, but no one has noticed that Mr. Hoop's Super Scoop is sometimes there and sometimes not.

We return to the LBN headquarters with no more clues than we started off with.

I decide to review the film we've taken so far. Alex takes the tape out of his camera and pops it into the VCR.

I watch Joshua, Amy, and me walk down the street, turn right, and then turn right again.

I watch Amy order her ice-cream cone.

And I watch as we leave the store.

So far nothing seems unusual—except for the eating habits of the Becker family.

On the tape, Amy is licking her Peppermint Bubblegum ice cream when suddenly Ms. Blanco and her plants appear. "Alex," I say, "why is the Garden Clock story on the same tape as the missing ice-cream parlor story?"

"I only had one tape left," he says.

I make a note: "Remind the LBN executives"—also known as Mom and Dad—"to buy more videotapes."

"Fast forward, Alex," I say. "I don't think we have enough *time* to review Ms. Blanco's Garden Clock story. Ha! Get it? Time? Garden Clock?"

Alex rolls his eyes. It's a good thing he's a great photographer.

I watch the second trip to the ice-cream parlor and my interviews with the neighbors.

But I don't see any more clues than I did before.

Nine

The Cold, Hard Facts

Back in my room, I take out my notebook and write down the facts of the case:

1. Joshua and Amy went to Mr. Hoop's Super Scoop Thursday afternoon.
2. Friday morning, when Amy and Dakota went, it wasn't there.
3. Mr. Hoop's Super Scoop was back in place a few hours later when the LBN news team joined Joshua and Amy to investigate.
4. Saturday morning, when Amy and Dakota went, it was missing again.

5. But it was there when the LBN news team arrived for the second time later that day.
6. Amy and Joshua Becker love ice cream.
7. Mr. Hoop loves free publicity.

I study the list. Could Amy and Joshua Becker love ice cream enough to steal a whole ice-cream shop?

No. That is impossible.

Could Mr. Hoop love publicity enough to make his ice-cream shop appear and disappear?

That is a possibility.

I study the list some more. But the cold, hard fact is: I just don't know the answer.

It is almost six o'clock and I still have no top story.

Suddenly, there is a knock on the garage door. I open it and find Mr. Hoop standing there. "I heard about your news show," he says. "And I thought you might want to hand these out to your viewers."

I look down at the stack of one-dollar-off coupons in his hand.

Normally, Lindy Blues would not consider giving out coupons during her news show. It is not very professional. But since I have not solved the mystery of the disappearing ice-cream shop, perhaps the coupons will satisfy my audience. "Thank you," I say.

He smiles. "Sorry I'll miss the show, but I have to get back to the shop."

As Mr. Hoop leaves, Joshua and Amy pass him on the way into the garage. Joshua's eyes are wide. "Did you solve the mystery? Did you make Mr. Hoop admit that he's the one who made the ice-cream shop disappear?"

I shake my head. "Sorry," I say. "All I got from Mr. Hoop were these coupons."

Amy takes a couple of coupons and tucks them in her pocket.

"I still think Mr. Hoop has something to do with it," Joshua says. "Maybe he's trying to throw us off the trail by giving out the coupons."

"Maybe," I say. "But it's almost time for the news, and the LBN news show must go on."

Soon the garage is full. All of my regular viewers are here. Ms. Blanco too. I have no choice but to play the tape and hope the answer to this mystery will come to me while I watch with my audience.

Alex presses the Forward button.

There is Friday's trip to Mr. Hoop's.

Ms. Blanco and her Garden Clock.

And then Saturday's trip to Mr. Hoop's.

As I watch the part where Joshua's ice-cream cone drips down his arm and onto my shoe, I see something that I did not notice before. "Alex!" I shout. "Freeze the tape!"

I turn to my audience. "You have seen two stories tonight—one of them about Mr. Hoop's Super Scoop and the other about

the biological clocks of plants and the mysterious ways their flowers open and close at different times of the day. In a strange and wonderful way, these two stories are related to each other. Can *you* solve the mystery of the disappearing ice-cream shop?"

Ten

Case Closed

The audience is silent. Even Ms. Blanco.

It is time for Lindy Blues to do something she has never done before. "I know you are all wondering exactly how Mr. Hoop's Super Scoop could disappear and then reappear for two days in a row," I say.

Everyone nods.

"In order to demonstrate the answer to this mystery, I am going to ask you to take a little trip with me."

I walk out the garage door and notice it is still light outside. I motion for my viewers to follow me. We all march down Flamingo

Road together. Except for Miranda Malone: She is walking on her hands.

We turn right at the end of the street and walk to the blue flowers where Alex filmed me cleaning my shoes.

I stop and turn to face my audience. "Do you all see these lovely blue flowers?" I ask. "Can anyone tell me what kind of flowers these are?"

Ms. Blanco raises her hand first. "They're morning glories," she says.

"Yes," I say. "And as we learned on tonight's news, because of their biological clocks, morning glories do not open their flowers until ten in the morning."

My viewers seem puzzled.

"Can anyone tell me what time Amy Becker walked to the ice-cream shop on Friday and Saturday mornings?"

Joshua raises his hand. "Eight thirty on Friday. Nine o'clock on Saturday."

"Thank you, Mr. Becker," I say. "That means when Amy Becker was walking with

68

her dog, Dakota, to the ice-cream shop on those two mornings, these flowers were not open."

My viewers still seem puzzled.

"Stay with me," I say. "Because Ms. Becker cannot read big words such as *Crocodile Road* or *Iguana Way*, she used blue flowers as her landmark. Because these flowers had not yet opened, she walked right past them and on to the next block."

There is whispering throughout the crowd.

"Let us walk another block together," I say.

When we get to the next block, I stop.

"Aha!" I say. "Just as I suspected." I point to the ground. "There are more blue flowers here."

I turn to Ms. Blanco. "I am going to guess that these blue flowers, which are not morning glories, are opened all the time. Is that right, Ms. Blanco?"

Ms. Blanco nods.

70

"I am also going to guess that when we turn onto this block we will find, not Mr. Hoop's Super Scoop, but a post office."

The crowd turns at the corner. And, sure enough, there's a post office.

"There it is," Amy says. "That's the post office I saw every morning."

"Yes," I say. "That is because every morning you walked one block too far. If you had waited until past ten o'clock to get ice cream, the morning glories would have been open and you would have turned at the correct street."

"But I was hungry before ten o'clock," Amy says.

"I understand," I say. "But in the future, it might be best to either wait until after ten o'clock to eat ice cream or find another landmark."

"Like what?" Amy says.

"Let's all go back to the morning glories and find one," I say.

As I examine the sidewalk next to the flowers, I notice there is something else Amy could use as a landmark. Melted ice cream. Lots of it. All over the sidewalk.

I point to the multicolored streaks of Rocky Road, Peppermint Bubblegum, and Mint Chocolate Chip ice cream. "Look," I say. "You can turn here next time."

Amy looks down.

"Unless, of course, it rains," I say. "Then you can you use the street sign as a landmark."

Amy looks up.

I point to the sign. "Mr. Hoop is on Croc-o-dile Way."

"Croc-o-dile Way," Amy says. "So if I turn here, I'll get to Mr. Hoop's Super Scoop no matter what time of day it is?"

"Yes you will."

Amy smiles. "So what are we waiting for?"

The crowd follows her around the corner. I realize I am losing my audience.

"Slow down," I say. "The LBN news is not over. I have one more surprise for you." I take the coupons out of my pocket and hand them out one at a time.

"Wow," Will Malone says. "This is the best news show ever."

"Yes it is," I say. "And, remember, join us next Saturday for another exciting broadcast of the LBN news. This is Lindy Blues, Your Nose for News."

My work is done.

Once we're all inside the shop, Mr. Hoop begins scooping ice cream like crazy and everyone is happy.

I look at Mr. Hoop and realize that he is a very nice man after all.

All of a sudden, I feel a tug on my jacket. It's Amy. "What about that box of popcorn you owe me?"

"Will you settle for an ice-cream cone?" I ask.

She nods.

I get a double scoop of Peppermint

Bubblegum for Amy and a double dip of French Vanilla for myself.

I take a lick.

Now this is one scoop I'm going to get to the bottom of. This is Lindy Blues, Your Nose for News, signing off with the sweet taste of success. Till next time.